YET I WILL REJOICE!

The Testimonies of Five Bible Personalities
Who Survived in Times of Doom and Despair

BOOK ONE

GOD ALONE
The Testimony of Rahab

JOHN REVELL

Life Line Press is an initiative of Life Line Chaplaincy, Inc.,
a 510(c)(3) not-for-profit corporation.

All profits go to help provide chaplaincy services for first
responders. For more information, go to LLChaplaincy.org.

Cover and book design by Rick Boyd, BOYDesign

Table of Contents

Introduction

*"Though the fig tree should not blossom, nor fruit be on the vines, the produce of the olive fail and the fields yield no food, the flock be cut off from the fold and there be no herd in the stalls, **yet I will rejoice in the Lord**; I will take joy in the God of my salvation. God, the Lord, is my strength; he makes my feet like the deer's; he makes me tread on my high places."*

HABAKKUK 3:17-19

The phrase, "yet I will rejoice" was first uttered by a Jewish prophet about 2,600 years ago. What makes it astounding—and particularly relevant for today—is that he wrote these words in the midst of civil and cultural chaos and demise. Even more incredible, God had just revealed to him that his nation was about to experience catastrophic collapse … everything was about to change in ways that he could never have imagined. Still, in the midst of frustration, angst, and perhaps even horror, he was able to stand and find cause for joy.

As I write, many are distraught over the prospect

of impending doom. We've entered an era that is entirely unfamiliar at least, unsettling at best, and perhaps unnerving for most. This current threat will diminish, but others are certain to follow—personally and individually, if not nationally or globally.

So, how are we to respond? How do we as God's people keep our wits about us while facing the prospect of such gloom and despair?

It may surprise you to know that throughout the Bible God's people often lived in dark times of uncertainty and under the prospects of doom. For many, it was the norm rather than the exception. In fact, many Christians throughout history have lived in such settings.

For many of us, especially in Western culture, it seems we've been spared—until now. Yet, God has not left us to face these dark days alone.

I would like to introduce you to five very special people from the Bible who faced the reality of impending doom and were drawn closer to God. Indeed, they were greatly used by God through their ordeals. Meet Rahab, Gideon, Jehoshaphat, Isaiah, and Habakkuk—ordinary people like you and me who faced extraordinary circumstances.

Through their ordeals, each one learned essential

lessons about God and faith, lessons that transcend the millennia to address our very fears and frustrations today.

As you read their stories in these five books you will likely find points at which you can identify with them. My hope and prayer is that you will recognize and benefit from the truths they came to understand and embrace.

In compiling these accounts I have been very careful to make sure the fictitious elements of the stories are entirely consistent with the biblical, historical, and archeological data. Of course there is a level of speculation inherent in such a work, but while I don't present every aspect of these accounts as *actual*, they are indeed presented as *plausible*.

Several who have read early copies have said they were compelled to reread the related portions of Scripture to determine the fiction level—I hope you will be so moved. We are not in His Word enough—if this meager offering moves any of us to deeper study and appreciation of the Bible, it will be a success. In fact, I pray these five books will help you discover and apply practical biblical principles for facing our current threats, but also that you will grow much deeper in your love for God and His Word.

CAUTION: The description of child sacrifice to Molech in Rahab's account is detailed and could be quite disturbing to parents and grandparents, especially of infants and young children. In such cases, it might be best to skip over this section. I thought about lessening the impact, but chose to proceed and include this advisory, because the material is essential for books four and five.

John Revell

Series Overview

The personal testimonies of a desperate prostitute, a terrified and broken warrior, a frantic king, a humble prophet who had seen God, and a frustrated prophet who had challenged God.

Yet I Will Rejoice is a series of five books providing the first-hand accounts of Rahab, Gideon, Jehoshaphat, Isaiah, and Habakkuk—five who were forced to face the very real prospect of doom, and who came to know, appreciate, and serve God more deeply as a result. This series attempts to convey timeless Bible lessons—lessons of faith, fortitude, courage, and obedience—that apply directly to those who live in alarming times.

Each book gives careful attention to relevant biblical, historical, cultural, and archeological details surrounding the character. It is written in a first-person style designed to illustrate the human frailties, fears, struggles and weaknesses of each biblical character, but even more demonstrate the consistency of God's plan and protection in the midst of fear and uncertainty.

RAHAB

BOOK ONE
God Alone
The Testimony of Rahab

Details the account of Rahab growing up as a sexually abused girl; then as a Canaanite prostitute in her father's Jericho inn; of her encounter with the Israelite spies; and of her eventual rescue from Jericho.

GIDEON

BOOK TWO
God, Are You Sure?
The Testimony of Gideon

Details the account of Gideon growing up in a home that was initially devoted to God, but that gradually was seduced by the lure of Canaanite idolatry, and then suffered seven years of attack by Mideonite Bedouin raiders. It also explores Gideon's pattern of fear, and God's patient and methodical transformation of a trembling, defeated man (likely crippled by PTSD) into a mighty warrior.

JEHOSHAPHAT

BOOK THREE
God, Help Us!
The Testimony of Jehoshaphat

Details the account of Jeho-shaphat's rise to power as king over Judah, his early dismal fail-ure in aligning with Ahab, and how he handled the threat of annihilation by enemy forces.

ISAIAH

BOOK FOUR
God With Us
The Testimony of Isaiah

Details the account of Isaiah's awesome vision of God; his call to ministry; his confrontation of a corrupt king and government; God's promise of deliverance from attack by northern forces; Isaiah's frustration over the ab-solute apostasy of Judah's king and government; and God's promise of a new future government.

BOOK FIVE

God, Why?
The Testimony of Habakkuk

Details Habakkuk's utter frustration over God's handling of Judah, focusing on the "golden years" under King Josiah, Josiah's devastating defeat and death on the battlefield, and the rise of the evil king Jehoiakim. This book reveals the level of disbelief, confusion, bitterness, and anger Habakkuk showed before God, and how God dramatically answered him, taking him to the point where he could experience joy even in the midst of the most catastrophic scenario imaginable.

CHAPTER 1

My Story

I knew the instant they walked through the door … they were different. These two men were not common merchants stopping at my inn for lodging—and whatever pleasures they might hope to find. Oh, they were dressed like the traders who would stay the night in Jericho en route to market their goods, but their faces were different—their eyes were not marked by the lust and greed I had come to expect from travelers. No, they were different.

Please forgive me; I have gotten ahead of myself. My name is Rahab. You may have heard of me with the label "prostitute" attached to my name. I was keeper of the inn on the north wall of Jericho. I must confess that I am embarrassed to admit my profession to you, but in the culture of Canaan it was not despised or shameful. Innkeepers were not wealthy, and in our situation the extra income from my prostitution helped provide food for my parents, brothers, and sisters.

But that very lifestyle may have made me even more aware of the difference I saw in those two when they walked through the door. Perhaps you might understand better if I told you some of my story ... and if you are facing dark days of doom and despair—as I was—perhaps my story will help.

My Background

My father purchased the inn when I was about 13. He had been a farmer, but a severe drought destroyed his crops one year, and he was forced to sell the field. He bought the inn, which was built into the walls that surrounded the city of Jericho in the land of Canaan, and he was able to barter with the king of Jericho who owned the fields around the city. My father would work a section of his fields in exchange for a small portion of the harvest each season.

It was during those days that I started down my dark path. Not long after we moved into the inn, my father allowed his own father to lie with me. That may sound unthinkable to you, but it was not uncommon for our culture. You see, the Canaanites believed their gods were moved to action based on the actions of people. Our main gods were El, Baal, Atar, and the Ammonite god Molech. Our main goddesses were Asherah, Anath, and Astarte—the goddesses of sex and war.

A major part of our belief in these gods and goddesses involved sex acts. We were taught that if we performed satisfactorily in their presence and pleased them, they might bless our crops, give us children, protect our health, and guard us from attacks by enemy forces.

It was common for relatives to lie with relatives—grandfathers with their granddaughters, sons with their mothers, and so on. If this did not move the gods to action, then some would even lie with animals. It is very difficult for me to talk about it now, but it was a way of life for us back then.

Times were very difficult; harvests had been lean, and my father thought that if he allowed his father to lie with me the gods might bless. So he did … but they did not.

My thoughts and feelings were all mixed up when

it happened that first time. I was terrified. It hurt so much … not just physically, but in so many different ways. I did not want to do it. I did not like it; in fact I hated it. I wept all that night and for many nights to come. But none of that mattered, because it was the way things were and would be. I was forced to accept it as what was needed for the good of the family.

Before that day, my father would catch my eye at times and smile at me. After that, he would not look into my eyes … and I do not remember him smiling at me again.

Something in me started dying that day.

If it had stopped then, I might have recovered; but it continued and even got worse—with my grandfather, then my uncles, and then with a lot of different men from the town. But the gods did not respond. Deep down I wondered what kind of gods these must be if they required this from me, but did nothing for us in return.

I started to sense a darkness growing in my heart—I had lost any of the happiness I knew in childhood. For some reason, I felt horribly guilty. Whatever had started to die inside that first time continued until gradually all light faded and disappeared.

Things got worse for my family. My father was

not making enough from the crops, so when I was in my late teens he decided the best way to make up for the loss was to sell my services to the travelers who stayed at the inn. I despised it.

My value was determined by my ability to satisfy the disgusting lusts of cruel men ... but there was nothing I could do. If I were to leave home, the only way I could survive as an unmarried woman would be as a prostitute. So why should I leave the safety of my home only to live the same life in isolation on the streets?

My lifestyle was not despised, but neither was it respected. None of the men from Jericho would ever want me for a wife, and it would have been too dangerous for me to leave home.

I realized I was trapped.

Over time, the despair grew more severe, and I sank into a deep pit of bitterness. I slowly stopped caring about anyone or anything.

Then my father became gravely ill. He was sick for a long time and could not work in the fields. My younger brothers were able to help some, but not enough to take care of the whole family.

So, I took charge of the inn. My mother and sisters would cook, clean, care for my father—and I would personally care for our customers.

I resigned myself to living this life. If this was the way it had to be, so be it. At least I was doing some good by helping my family survive. That thought might have been the only thing that got me through those dark days … and nights.

The Hittite Traders

But one day some Hittite traders stopped at the inn on their return trip to the coastal city of Joppa. They sailed down from the north each year bringing pots, knives, and metal tools to trade with the Babylonians and Arabs.

The road from Joppa was a trade route that crossed from the Great Sea on the western shore, through the range of hills, past Jericho at the eastern base of that range, through the Jordan River, and then connected to the King's Highway just to the east of the Jordan. That is where these Hittites met each year to trade for precious cloth and dyes from Babylon, or gold, incense, and ointments from Arabia.

Traveling merchants often stayed at our inn just inside the walls of Jericho. The city had two levels:

upper and lower. The upper section of the city had a high wall around it, and the wealthy of the city lived inside those walls. The poorer people of Jericho lived in the area around the perimeter below those walls and were surrounded by the second wall that had been built upon a high stone embankment circling the entire city. The design made it almost impossible for invading armies to storm the city. Our two-story inn was on the lower level of the north side of the city and had been built up against the lower wall, using it as the rear of our dwelling.

Returning Hittite traders sometimes would linger at Jericho and trade any remaining goods for salt and bitumen drawn from the Salt Sea by local merchants. Our inn was just inside the gate, not far down on the right, so it was easy for traders find us and tie their animals outside our door.

After these Hittites settled, they started talking about the Israelites. The people of Jericho were always interested in the latest on these wandering 12 Tribes because we had been hearing for years that they were coming our way. For almost 40 years the rumor had grown that they would invade the land of Canaan and destroy us.

I was skeptical. You know how rumors are. Even

if the Israelites did invade, I did not really care—it would probably be better if we were all killed. In fact, I would take great delight in watching certain men suffer, scream, and perish by the blade of an Israelite … or by any blade.

Before long, a group had gathered at the inn to listen as the Hittites spoke of when the Israelites had come up the King's Highway from the south, passing through Moab until they came to the land of the Amorites. They had sent messengers to Sihon, the Amorite king, asking permission to pass through and promising not to harm the land or the people.

Sihon was a stubborn man (which we had known for years), but very powerful—probably the most powerful king in that area. He refused permission and gathered his troops to face the Israelites, only to be utterly destroyed. Then the Israelites took over the entire land! Every city!

They did not stop there. They continued further north and conquered King Og and the land of Bashan. Not one of his soldiers survived the battle.

The Hittites said they kept hearing that the Israelite god, *Yahweh*, was responsible for the victories. This was not a new name for us. The people of Canaan had heard of him 40 years earlier after the Israelites departed Egypt. Every trader from the south had repeated the story over and over again of how *Yahweh* had struck the Egyptians, delivered the Israelites from slavery, parted the Red Sea so they could pass through, then drowned the Egyptian army when they tried to chase after them.

Panic slowly overcame the crowd. What if the rumors were true? What if they were not satisfied to stay east of the Jordan, but crossed over to invade *our* land? Years ago traders had repeated portions of a victory song from their leader, Moses. The portion that lingered in everybody's ear was:

> *The peoples have heard; they tremble;*
> > *pangs have seized the inhabitants of Philistia.*
> *Now are the chiefs of Edom dismayed;*
> > *trembling seizes the leaders of Moab;*
> > *all the inhabitants of Canaan have melted*
> > *away.*
> *Terror and dread fall upon them;*
> > *because of the greatness of your arm*
> > *they are still as stone.*

Someone in the crowd mentioned that song and suddenly everyone was still. Then they all raced out of the inn and scattered to spread the news.

But as the people started talking and worrying, I started thinking. Here is a god who can conquer mighty armies and even parted the Red Sea. Our gods could not even deliver my family from poverty. I was afraid to tell anybody, but long ago I had secretly started to hate these gods.

Every time I was forced to lie with my father's father, or his brothers, or the men of the city, I blamed the gods for letting me suffer—no, for actually *causing* my suffering.

And the suffering did not stop with me. I knew of other women, and even children, who were hurt by these horrible acts. There were priests and kings who believed that if some of the people sacrificed their first-born child to the god Molech, he would give them wisdom and guidance.

So I wondered, "If these gods are so good, why do so many people suffer so much as a result of worshipping them. If these gods have any power, why do they not bless our crops and families? It does not make sense.

"At the same time, here is a nation that follows a god who clearly is very powerful. This god even cared enough for his people to deliver them from slavery to the Egyptians! Imagine that—worshipping and following a powerful and good god!"

Well, I put that thought aside. I knew I would never have the chance to follow him. If all of the stories were right, we would all be destroyed anyway … which I thought would likely be best for us all.

The Hittites departed the next day, leaving a murmuring, anxious city behind.

A SPARK OF HOPE

Two days later, another group of traders stopped by the inn. They, too, had word of the Israelites, but nothing new so no one pushed them for details. But later that night, I listened from the shadows at the other end of the room as one shared about his recent visit with relatives who had joined the Israelites. It seemed the nation would allow outsiders (they referred to them as "aliens") to join them if they would agree to follow *Yahweh* and all of his teachings.

Up to that point I was not paying much attention, but when I heard that, I moved a bit closer and tried to listen without being noticed. The other men laughed and asked why his relatives would want to join such an odd group who followed only one god—a god who prohibited them from enjoying life. Worshipping Baal gave so much more pleasure (when I heard that, I wanted to shout, "Perhaps for the men, but not for women and children!" But I knew better than to express my thoughts).

Yet he defended his relatives. He said they told him some very curious things about following *Yahweh*. This god had made a covenant to bless and protect his people if they would remain faithful and true to him alone. He expected them to tell the truth, to be faithful to their spouses, to protect and care for the helpless. He commanded them to love him completely, and to love their neighbors as they would themselves, and he assured them of his own love and tender mercies.

The trader also talked about their sacrifices, that each year the high priest would take two goats. One he would kill as payment for the peoples' sin, and the other he would symbolically place the people's sin upon its head and then send it out into the wilderness as a picture of their sin being removed from them.

He went on to talk more about his relatives,

but I stopped listening. His comments had become lodged in my mind. A god who cared for the helpless, one who emphasized true love and concern for each other, one who actually loved them and removed their sin from them.

Something ignited inside me right then—something I had not felt for years—a spark of *hope*. I realized what had died inside me years earlier—it indeed was hope. Could it be that this God truly cared for people? Was it possible that He really prompted love and concern for others? Could such a God actually remove sin from people's lives? Could He take away my own guilt, my own darkness?

And this traveler talked about "aliens." Could it be that He really allowed others to join the nation? I wondered … if I were to sneak out of Jericho and cross the Jordan and find them, maybe they would—maybe **He** would let me ….

I immediately stopped my thoughts. I should have known better than to let them run away; it could only lead to more disappointment and despair. I could not leave my family; they would be helpless. Besides, after the life I had lived I was certain He would not receive me or allow me to become one of His people.

That night I fell into bed frustrated and angry.

CHAPTER 2

The Spies

A Surprise Visit

The city continued to buzz for some time. Were the Israelites going to cross the Jordan? If they were coming, when would it be? But winter passed and harvest time approached, and everyone started to relax a bit. As the snows from the northern mountains melted, the waters of the Jordan would rise. Combined with the spring rains, it would be impossible for so many people to cross with all of their livestock, tents, and supplies. They would likely stay encamped where they were a few months longer, giving the city until mid-to-late summer to prepare and barricade itself.

Spring came, and with it the harvest of flax from the fields (our crops grew in late winter and early spring, and were harvested in late spring). My brothers worked hard and did very well. The king's steward who oversaw the fields allowed us a few extra bundles as a bonus—of course he would also expect *me* to personally reward him.

We would sell the flax at market to the weavers who would beat it and weave it into fine linen. We stored the bundles on the flat roof of our house, against the outer wall, stacked neatly so they would dry in the sun.

Then, late one afternoon those two men walked through the door. As I said earlier, they were different. When I walked up to them they did not stare at me like other men would; neither of them had that typical disgusting smirk on their faces. They did not glare at me. Neither of them reached out to grab me and snatch me up against his body. One looked to be about my age, the other a little younger.

I instantly thought of the Israelites! What if these two are spies who had somehow made it across the Jordan? My heart started pounding as excitement began to well up inside.

So I approached cautiously, looked into their eyes, and whispered, "Are you Israelites?"

Their expressions were a combination of alarm

and curiosity. I think they were alarmed that some-one had identified them, but seemed curious at how I acted toward them. I was visibly excited, but not alarmed or hostile, which is probably what they would expect.

The older one admitted (under his breath) they were; then he looked at me and asked softly, "Why you are smiling?"

I suddenly realized the danger they faced. We had no time for details. I grabbed their arms and said, "Come with me! NOW!!" I made sure no one was looking and pulled them up the ladder to the room above, then over to the ladder that went up to the roof. When we got to the roof I directed them to lay over against the wall, then I covered them with the bundles of flax.

I warned them, "No matter what happens, do not move! Do not make any noise, or we could all die! I will return for you when it is safe."

My Dilemma

As soon as I stepped off the bottom rung of the lad-der, panic began to sweep over me. I knew someone would have seen them come in and suspect they were not traders—they had no camels or donkeys—and they clearly were not from Jericho, so it was only a matter of time before the guards would come.

What was I going to do? If the guards found them I would die—my whole family would die! And that tortuous death would be more terrible than I could imagine. Their pattern from of old was, "maximum pain, blood, screams, horror ... and then slow death."

I could not bear to see my father and mother tortured. Yes, he had given me over when I was a child, but I really do not believe he knew any better. And years later, when he saw what had happened to me, I think I sensed a measure of regret and sorrow deep in his eyes.

He never allowed my younger sisters to go through what I experienced. I think it was because he saw what had gradually happened to me. If discovered, the soldiers would humiliate and torture him and my mother before they slowly killed them both.

Then they would take my brothers and sisters and their families. One of my brothers had married and had a child, and one of my sisters also had married. They would all be put to death; and they would all

look to me—I would be forced to watch them die—
then I would be put to the sword.

I thought, "Maybe I should get the guards right
now. If I did, I would be a hero! They might even
give us a reward. I would not have to sell myself any
more. We could buy another farm and get away from
the city. We could hire workers for the field, so my
father would not have to worry any more.

"Maybe I could even find a man who did not
know about my past, a man who would marry me—
and hold me, and protect me—a man who might actually love me and not just use me...."

Then I stopped my thoughts and remembered
... these men followed *Yahweh*. He repeatedly had
shown Himself to be a good God. He clearly cared
for His people more than our gods cared for us.

That is when the truth broke down the door of
my mind and overtook me. Our gods were not what
the priests had said! If they really existed, they did
not care about these people, they never helped my
family, and they certainly did not care for me. They
were powerless, and following them led to my life of
misery. In fact, following them destroyed the lives of
countless others in the land.

In contrast, *Yahweh* delivered His people from

slavery, provided for and protected them for forty years, and was about to give them a new land. Also, *Yahweh* had **real** power. If He could defeat Pharaoh, part the Red Sea and destroy the Egyptian army with it, and defeat Sihon and Og, then Jericho could never stand against Him. Indeed, the old song said He was going to deliver all of Canaan over to the Israelites. The truth was these false gods would be powerless to stop Him!

What if the two spies were able to escape and return to the Israelites? Maybe, I thought, if I protect them they will agree to spare us when they attack. Maybe they would accept us into the community like they did with other aliens.

Maybe we would even be allowed to follow and worship *Yahweh*.

I did not want to let my hopes run away, but right then I knew that I **had** to protect them. If *Yahweh* were anything like what we heard, He would be able to protect us in return.

Then I stopped, thought for a moment, and decided: even if He chose not to protect us, I would rather die helping Him take the land, than die helping the gods of this land.

The Guards

At that instant, there was violent pounding on the main door. I ran over and opened the door to find the king's guards. They said someone had seen two Israelite spies come into the inn and demanded to come in and search. They did not await my response but burst in, shoving me aside. They started on the first level, going room to room, throwing baskets and bedding aside, looking everywhere. Then they climbed the ladder to the second level.

My heart was pounding the whole time, but I tried not to let it show. As I followed them throughout, I told them that the two had indeed been there earlier, but that I did not know who they were or where they had come from. Then I told them they had left just a few moments earlier at dusk, and that if they hurried they could probably catch them. Of course they did not find anything on the second level, so they climbed the ladder to the roof.

As we were climbing anxiety almost overcame me; I could feel my heart pounding hard against my chest. It was so loud, I was afraid they would be able to hear it. They started kicking at some of the bundles of flax, and just as they were about to kick the stack covering the Israelites I screamed frantically, "Listen! I told you that they just left! You have to hurry, or they will get away! Do you want the king to hear you let them escape? If you go right now you still might catch them!"

They stopped, looked at each other, pushed me aside, and rushed down both ladders and out the main door. I followed them down and listened through the window by the door as they gathered supplies and then ran out through the city gate. I heard the gatekeepers slam the gate and put the huge wooden crosspiece in place to lock it.

THE ARRANGEMENT

I collapsed on a stool by the door and put my head back against the wall. After catching my breath and waiting a few minutes to make sure they were gone, I climbed back up to the roof and spoke softly to the spies through the bundles of flax. I told them that the guards had left, but that they needed to remain hidden for a short time just to be safe, and that I would be back later with something to eat.

After making certain the guards would not return, I helped the two spies climb out from under the flax. I gave them each food and drink, then sat silently and watched them as they ate. Shortly one of them, the older one, said, "You knew who we were. Why did you hide us?"

So I explained that I understood *Yahweh* was going to give our land to the Israelites and that the whole city, indeed all of Canaan, knew they were coming. Everyone was terrified—it's as if their hearts were melting. I told them that I had heard of how *Yahweh* had delivered their people from slavery in Egypt, how He parted the Red Sea, and how He completely destroyed Sihon and Og.

I also explained that I heard He would even receive aliens.

I continued, telling them I realized how this God was the only true God, the God over all the heavens, and the God over all the earth.

Immediately, as soon as those words left my lips, I felt something rush through my heart. I cannot fully explain it, but for the very first time a surprising sense of peace started sweeping over and through me. The tightness in my stomach started to ease, my shoulders relaxed a little, and my neck began to loosen. But there was also an incredible sense of something else welling up inside—it was the *hope* I sensed weeks earlier—far more than I had as a child, far more than I lost as a teen. Then I felt a joy start to rise up inside like I had never known. There were times when I was happy as a child, but I had never known what I was starting to feel.

They also knew something was happening inside me—they could see it in my face—but there is no way they could have understood it.

But I could not stop to think about it; I had to tell them more. I hurried to remind them that I showed them kindness and faithfulness, so I expected them to show the same by sparing my life and the lives of all of my family when they destroyed the city.

They swore and gave me specific instructions. They told me to keep silent about their visit, and they gave me a scarlet cord, instructing me to hang it in the window of the second floor on the outside wall so the Israelites would know which house was mine. If I did not, and if all of my family members were not in the house at the time of the attack, they could not be held responsible for the outcome.

I agreed, and then I let them down with a rope through that outside window. I warned them to hide in the hills to the west for three days until the guards returned. They slid down the rope, and I watched as they gradually disappeared into the darkness.

Then I attached that scarlet cord outside the window.

CHAPTER 3

The March

WHAT THE SHEPHERDS SAW

The guards returned the three days later without finding the spies—to my relief. They had gone eastward along the road down to the Jordan, then up and down the west bank of the river, but found nothing. They reported that because the river was running so high, it was unlikely the two men were Israelites as it would have been too difficult for them to cross it. Even if they were, the Israelites would not be able to cross that river for several weeks.

Everyone relaxed some, but the priests of the city called for a ceremony of protection that night in which the people would call on the god Attar and the goddess Anath and offer them sacrifices—as a precaution. They reminded everyone that if the people were willing to please their gods, these gods would stand up and defeat this *Yahweh*—or any other god who would dare to attack their city.

The night was filled with the awful noise of desperate people gathered as a mob at the city's altar to plead with and appease their gods. As part of the ritual some would lie with each other, while the rest of the town—men, women, and children—danced and sang around them. I watched as one man approached another and led him to the center. An older man came out of the crowd and took the hand of a teenage girl, likely his granddaughter. It was obviously her first time. She hesitated and looked back at her mother who just turned and looked at the ground. My chest felt heavy—I hurt deeply for her.

I had seen this all of my life, and had even participated more times than I wished to remember, so I was surprised when this made me uncomfortable. I wanted to go home but I was afraid if I left someone might become suspicious.

I knew the people were wasting their time. Their gods would not hear and could not act.

How tragic … how sad: people crying out to the very gods that were destroying them, seeking deliverance and protection from the only God who could save them.

The next day, the people were exhausted, but seemed a little less anxious.

But, a few days later the city erupted in chaos. I heard the commotion and went out into the center of town to see what was happening. Three local shepherds had run into the city screaming, "They're coming! They're coming! The Israelites, they're coming!!!"

Instantly they were surrounded by a mob shouting at them, asking about the Israelites. Everyone was screaming a different question and the men, who were already shaken and breathing heavily, were confused and did not know which questions to answer first. Some of the upper level residents and priests started coming down to see what the disturbance was about. Finally one of the priests shouted for everyone to be quiet and let them tell their story.

As the crowd quieted down, the shepherds explained:

"We were up close to Gilgal with our sheep," said one, "and this morning as we moved the sheep toward the river we heard a faint rumbling noise in the distance. At first we thought it was just the sound of the river, but it kept getting louder."

"That's right," said another, "then as we got closer

to the river, we saw a small cloud of dust above the eastern plain of the Jordan. It almost looked like a dust storm, but different somehow, it was not big enough. Then, we could hear the faint sound of livestock—sheep, goats, and cattle—off in the distance. We looked at each other and started walking a little slower. As the sun rose higher we could see through the dust, and it looked like the ground on the other side of the river was moving—as far as we could see. The closer we got to the river, the louder the sound. Then, when we reached the edge of the plateau and looked down to the river we just couldn't believe what we saw!"

A hush suddenly fell on the crowd.

"What was it???" someone yelled.

The first shepherd spoke again. "There, over on the east bank, was a sea of people with all of their livestock and belongings—as far as you could see." The other shepherds nodded in agreement, their eyes opened wide. "We knew it was the Israelites! There was a cloud of dust all around them as they slowly made their way toward the river. I've never seen anything like it."

"That's right," added the third, "And way out in front there were some men carrying poles that held a big box with two gold figures—or statues, or something—on top. And right above that box was a strange column of smoke—or cloud—I'm not sure what it was—that reached up to the heavens. I've never seen anything like that in all my life!"

"Then the four men with the box started walking toward the river with that column of cloud above them," said the second shepherd. "And they just kept walking like they were going to walk into the river, and we all looked at each other, and our eyes got bigger, and then we looked back at them, and, and, … and they just kept walking, right down to the river!!! And I just knew they were going to die, because, you know, it was at full flood stage!

"But they didn't!" said the first. "As soon as the feet of the first two touched the edge of water, the river started going down. And they kept walking down toward the middle, and the water kept receding down toward the normal riverbanks, then below them! By the time they got to the middle of the riverbed, the river had stopped flowing completely!!!"

A woman in the crowd shrieked, several gasped, and everyone started mumbling. He spoke again, "The men holding the box on the poles with the gold statues and the column of cloud over it stopped right

in the middle of the riverbed. And then all of the Israelites started walking down into the riverbed and
crossing to this side. And that's when we took off
running."

PANIC

The whole crowd panicked. Some were screaming, some were crying—chaos started to spread
throughout the city.

I knew I could not let it show, but inside I was
thrilled.

Then one of the priests stepped forward and
shouted at them, "How dare you doubt the power of
Molech!!!"

Everyone grew silent.

"This *Yahweh* can be no match for Molech," he
proclaimed. "Do not fear! He will care for us. But you
know what we must do—we must sacrifice to him.
Decide which of you will have the honor of making
the sacrifice, then gather at the shrine tonight!

"Dare not doubt the power of Molech!"

I turned around and made my way back to my
home—and shuddered as I thought of what was ahead.

That night I walked with my mother and father, along with the entire city, out to the shrine of Molech. It was on the top of the grassy ridge just west of the city. There, a tall, hollow bronze statue of Molech stood facing the city, his arms stretched out in front of him. A fire was already raging at the base of the statue, its flames rising past his arms to just below his ugly head.

Again, I did not want to be there, but I was afraid if I stayed back, the king and his guards might become suspicious.

The priests were lined up behind the shrine, beating their drums in time with each other and singing a low, monotone, somber chant. The reflection from the flames danced across their faces, giving them a mysterious and fearsome appearance.

As the crowd gathered, the priest who had spoken earlier in town began the ceremony. He chanted, and then prayed that Molech would hear their prayers, receive their offering, and protect Jericho from the invading god, *Yahweh*. He asked Molech to show his strength so that Jericho and all of Canaan, indeed so that every land, would know that Molech was the true king of all gods.

The drums picked up their beat, a little faster

now, as all the priests began crying out to Molech. The head priest started pacing back and forth before the crowd, shouting at first, and then screaming praises to Molech. Soon the crowd joined him, a little hesitant at first, but then with more and more confidence.

The volume of the drums and the crowd kept rising and rising, growing to a deafening level. It stopped all at once when the head priest reached down, picked up a long pole with a metal basket hanging on the end, and lifted it up into the dark night sky. He then turned and walked to the crowd and put the basket on the ground.

At that moment a couple stepped forward holding their young infant son. I was too far back to see their faces. The priest took the baby from their arms and lifted him up above his head for the crowd to see—they cheered wildly. He then put the baby in the basket and picked it up with the pole.

The people started chanting the name of Molech as the priest approached the statue. I turned my head at that point—I had seen it many times before—I could not bear to watch the horror and add to the images that haunt me to this day. Right then, the drums pounded louder and faster, and the people all started cheering so loud my ears hurt.

After a moment the priest held up his hands for silence. When the drums and chanting stopped, he paused and said, "Molech is well pleased. Fear not for your safety, nor for your city. He will protect."

The people cheered and started dancing and singing in celebration. My stomach felt sick as I turned and headed back toward the inn.

I could not sleep that night.

The next few days passed without any news. The shepherds reported that the Israelites had camped at Gilgal and they did not see much activity, especially by the men. The king had ordered the gates to be closed and no one was allowed to enter or leave. I told my father and mother, as well as my brothers and sisters and their families that when the Israelites came I thought the safest place for us all would be the inn. I did not explain why, and they could not understand my persistence, but I continued begging them until they all agreed to come.

The Israelite Army

Then one morning there was a great deal of noise and activity outside our main door. Watchmen on the northeast corner tower shouted that they could see the Israelites coming our direction. The guards put additional wooden beams, as thick as young trees, across the gates to secure them. They placed more ladders up against the lower wall on both sides of the gate so they could view down the steep embankment below. Then the soldiers, with their spears and swords, ran to their positions by the gate and at several points around the wall in case the Israelites broke through.

I was both excited and frightened at the same time. This was the day my family and I would be delivered! I told my parents and two youngest brothers and sister to stay there while I raced to find my other brother and sister and hurry them and their families to my house.

We ran inside, secured the door, and all climbed up the ladder to the second floor so we could watch through the outside window. I glanced outside just below the window to make sure the scarlet cord was secure.

Then we waited—but not for long. We could hear them long before we could see them. There was a low, rumbling sound like what the shepherds described. It must have been the noise from their feet as thousands of soldiers marched our way. Then I heard trumpets playing in the distance. The noise got louder and louder, and actually we saw them through our window coming from the northeast—then, as they got closer I could see them more clearly—thousands of armed soldiers marching side by side, looking straight ahead.

As they approached and passed below my window, I realized that they looked different than any soldiers I had ever seen. Despite the clouds of dust swirling about, I could see that they all looked so noble, brave, and ... virtuous, as they passed beneath our window along the northern wall. The scene moved me in ways I cannot describe.

Then I saw it! Behind the soldiers were seven men in robes playing trumpets made from rams' horns; behind them came four men carrying the two gold poles that held the large box. It was just as the shepherds described. The top of the box was covered with gold. At each end there was a gold statue of a man in a robe. Each man was on his knees facing toward the center, but they each had wings coming from their backs that were also pointed toward the middle.

Rising out from the center of the box, between those gold wings, there was the pillar of cloud the shepherds had described—it reached up to the heavens. It was unlike anything I had ever seen in my life. As it passed beneath my window, tears came to my eyes and my throat hurt when I tried to swallow. I cannot describe how I felt—it was a sense of awe that was completely new to me. This most certainly must be *Yahweh,* at last!

Eventually I came to understand that *Yahweh* is far too great to have been confined to a mere pillar of cloud or fire, and that this was just the way in which He appeared to the Israelites to demonstrate His presence. But even if I had known the larger truth at the time, it would not have mattered. What I saw was so different from the lifeless statues of the Canaanite gods with such angry and cruel faces. This pillar was so splendid, so magnificent, so breathtaking—and so humbling. I would have fallen to my knees, but I could not take my eyes off the sight.

It passed with throngs of soldiers following. They all walked past our window marching to the northwest corner of the city. I kept waiting for the battle cry, but it never came. I went down to the first-floor window by the main door to listen. I could hear the priests in the center of the city's upper level; they were screaming, praying, and chanting to the gods. Then some soldiers reported that the Israelites had circled around the northwest corner and were marching along the western wall.

Soon the guards on the ladders at the southwest corner reported that they were coming their way—and then the army turned and marched along the southern end to the southeast corner. After a bit, the guards reported that the army was marching along the eastern wall back toward the northeast corner. But then … everyone was amazed to hear that they were turning slightly to the right and starting back toward Gilgal and the river! I could actually see them as they marched away.

I cannot explain the feelings of despair and panic that started to overcome me as I watched *Yahweh* leave. One of the guards warned that it might be a trick, but they looked on—as did I from my window—while the last Israelite soldier disappeared over the horizon.

The city erupted in cheers.

My heart sank as I watched them all leave me.

The priests said their gods, especially Molech, faced *Yahweh* and turned him back! The single Israelite god was no match for all of their gods!

My brother and sister and their families returned to their homes. The rest of the day I struggled. If *Yahweh* was as strong as I believed, why did He not take the city? They did not even attack—they just marched around the city! Did I put my family at risk for nothing? Had I made the right decision?

Even worse, and troubling down to my very soul, I fought the feeling that perhaps I had been overlooked—even betrayed—by yet another god. As everyone celebrated later, I fought the despair of being abandoned and stranded in the life I so desperately wanted to escape. That night was darker than any I could remember.

But the next morning I thought that this might perhaps be part of a plan. Maybe He had the Israelites march around the city to look for weaknesses in the wall. Maybe He was not defeated at all! Then I heard the trumpets in the distance. My heart started pounding inside again. I ran and gathered my family members again and rushed them to the inn. The priests were urging everyone to pray to the gods and trust them again. When we got upstairs I waited by the window to watch for them.

"Maybe today," I thought.

The Israelites approached and circled the city the same as the day before—then turned back toward the river again.

The priests and people celebrated their gods again, mocking *Yahweh's* weakness and the Israelites' foolishness for trusting him alone. One priest tried to balance their insults, pointing out that *Yahweh* was obviously a powerful god—look at what he did to the Red Sea and to the Jordan. It is just that He could not overpower the combined strength of all the gods when they joined forces to protect their faithful followers. He stressed that this should be a lesson for everyone in Jericho—no, to everyone in Canaan—that if the people remained faithful to their gods, no one could destroy them.

I was confused, but not as discouraged as the day before.

The scene was repeated again each day for the next four days. Each time, the people of Jericho became increasingly confident so that by the sixth day the guards relaxed on their ladders and laughed at the Israelites as they marched around the city. They even shouted down insults, mocking the god of Israel and those who would trust him.

But with each day I became more and more discouraged. I gradually returned to my thoughts of the first day. If He was that strong, why had He not taken the city? What if there was some truth to what the priests were saying? What if the combined strength of all the gods were more powerful than He?

"If that is true," I thought, "then I will never get out of here." At that point, anguish overtook me, and the remnants of that newfound hope began to crumble. As I lay down that night, I started to fear it might all have been a big lie, that all we had heard over the years might have been unfounded legends. I began to suspect that if *Yahweh* were real, He probably was not able to overcome the combined power all of the gods.

Even worse, I knew I was doomed, because eventually the king would discover my role, and my family would pay the price. Graphic images of my family screaming in agony as they were being tortured and executed kept repeating in my mind, tormenting me the rest of that sleepless night.

THE SEVENTH DAY

When I heard the trumpets early on the seventh day I did not gather my family as quickly as six days earlier—and when I did, they were not as quick to respond. Though we could hear and feel the rumble of their marching again, some of the guards did not even take their posts along the wall.

The guards already on the ladders were more annoyed than alarmed. The priests said that maybe after today, the Israelites would finally understand and give up. One spoke of the opportunity to introduce the Israelites to the gods of Canaan, that after today they might be ready to turn from *Yahweh*; or at least be open to worshipping the gods of Canaan in addition to *Yahweh*.

My family did not even go with me to the second-floor window this time. I watched as the army marched past, then I watched as the gold box and *Yahweh* passed by. Deep in my heart I still longed for Him to deliver my family and me, and for the Israelites to destroy the city, but I no longer expected it. After they all passed I slowly walked across the room and dropped down on a stool. Resting my head back against the wall, I glanced over at the crimson cord in the window and wondered why I had even left it there after the first day.

I leaned forward, crossed my arms across my knees, and dropped my forehead down onto my arms.

I do not remember how long I sat there—it could not have been too long—but after a while I heard a disturbance. I hurried down the ladder and saw my family all crowded around the window by the main door. The guard on the ladder at the northeast corner had screamed that the Israelites were not turning back to the Jordan. Instead they were rounding the corner and marching along the northern wall! The guards all started running to their posts along the walls. I ran back up the ladder and to the window.

There they were! They were coming right toward me. They passed outside my window again, just like the first time. I began to get excited again. Maybe this was truly the time.

They kept going, and then came around a third time. The guards were no longer annoyed, now they were alert.

They passed a fourth time then started the fifth. With each pass I got more excited. My father and brothers had come upstairs with me and were struggling to see out the window. I ran down the ladder to check on my mother and sisters. They were terrified. I drew them close to me, put my arms around them, and whispered that everything would be okay, that they would be safe. They pulled back and looked into my eyes with confused expressions. I told them that I would explain later but that for now they had no reason to worry.

I climbed back up the ladder, and my father walked in my direction—still looking over his shoulder toward the window—and said they had just passed a sixth time. He glanced at me briefly, then stopped and looked back toward me again and caught my eyes … something he had not done in many years. He stared at me in amazement. I realized I was smiling. I rushed over to him and hugged him. It was the first time we had embraced since I was a child.

At first he was surprised and stood stiffly, not sure how to respond; but he slowly put his arms around me loosely, and then he pulled me close and held me tightly in his arms. Tears filled my eyes—for the first time that I could remember in years—and I felt him catch a quick breath and start to sob. He continued to hold me tightly, and we stood there for a moment, a moment for which I had deeply longed for many, many years. Then I whispered in his ear, "*Yahweh* will save us." He pushed back from me, and through his tears he looked at me with surprise—and a glimmer of hope flashed through his eyes.

The oldest of my brothers called back to us that they were passing for the seventh time. Just then I noticed a little dust and dirt falling from the ceiling. I pulled away from my father and walked over to the window to watch.

They disappeared again around the northwest wall, so we left the window for a moment. My oldest brother looked at me and asked why I was so happy when it looked like the Israelites were finally about to do something. I told him to just wait and he would see for himself.

My mother, sisters, and nephew climbed up the ladder to see what the Israelites were doing. We explained that they had passed for the seventh time and that by now they were probably along the southern wall. Then everyone stopped and stared at me. My mother asked, "Rahab, why are you so excited? Why do you think everything will be alright?"

I paused, looked at them, took a breath, paused again, and then spoke. "Two Israelite spies came to the inn about three weeks ago. I hid them from the guards. I did not tell you because I did not want to put you in any danger."

The older of my sisters gasped and put her hand over her mouth. My brothers' eyes grew large, and their mouths opened wide in disbelief. I continued, "*Yahweh*, the God of the Israelites, will destroy Jericho, but the spies have promised to save us. He parted the Red Sea, destroyed the Egyptian army, brought the Israelites through the wilderness, and destroyed Og and Sihon and all of their armies. You know the old song—they will destroy Jericho. But we will be safe. We will be able to join the Israelites—and follow their God—the only true God."

THE ATTACK

As I finished that statement we heard the army arriving outside the window below the embankment. We all crowded around to get a better view. Then the Israelites stopped. The silence seemed strange following all of the marching and trumpet blasts.

I wondered for a moment how they would attack with no ladders.

A man who looked older than the rest, but strong, walked out in front of them up to the top of a small ridge next to them. The whole army, stationed together along the base of the embankment, looked at him and listened. We could not hear very well from our window, but I heard him say the words "shout" and "consecrate." Then we all heard him say my name. Immediately my whole family turned to me with wide eyes.

Suddenly, the trumpets started playing again—this time in long, sustained blasts—and all the Israelite soldiers and priests began to shout. The sound was deafening. We all had to put our hands over our ears.

The shouting and trumpet blasts continued, and I began to wonder why they would do this before rushing the walls. And where were their ladders?

Then the floor started trembling slightly. We all looked at each other without speaking. Dust started to fall from the ceiling as the shouting continued. The floors stopped trembling for a moment, and then started again. Then it turned to rumbling, and the floor and walls started shaking violently.

I yelled for everyone to run down the ladder. The walls started to sway in and out, chunks of dirt fell from the ceiling, then we heard a terrible rumbling sound outside. I was the last one down, and as I stepped off the ladder the roof above the second-floor ceiling caved in.

Dirt and debris crashed through the opening above us sending a smothering cloud of dirt and dust through the room, but the floor above us remained—for the moment. We all huddled together on the floor along the back wall, opposite the main door.

The ground beneath us seemed to roll as chunks of dirt from the ceiling above fell on us.

All at once, on both sides of our house, we heard a mighty crashing sound. The guards on the ladders by the gate screamed, but were suddenly silenced. Then the sound moved out away from each side of the house, extending in opposite directions.

The crashing sound continued all around the whole city—and then it stopped. At the same time the trembling and rolling beneath us ceased.

Outside our door we could hear screaming, shouting, and crying. The Israelites continued to shout, but we could tell they had begun moving up into the city. I could not understand how that was possible, because they were so far below the embankment with no ladders. Before long, the sound of Israelites shouting filled the city. People were running everywhere and we heard the terrible noise of battle. Throughout the city swords were clashing—and people were dying.

A fight started right outside our main door. Some of the soldiers from Jericho were calling out the names of Molech, Baal, and Atar. Israelites came upon them and they fought violently. Someone crashed up against our door—I thought it was going to collapse—then again. More yelling, then another body slammed against the door.

For a moment I starting to panic, thinking the Israelites might not spare us.

Then silence.

Suddenly, the door burst open. My sister screamed. Two Israelite soldiers ran toward us with swords in hand. I reached across to shield my parents.

They stopped, and one stooped down toward us and reached out his hand.

"Rahab, come quickly," he said. I looked in his face and then recognized him as the older of the two Israelite spies. The soldier with him was the younger spy.

He took my hand and pulled me to my feet, and instantly I threw my arms around him and held him tightly. But he grabbed my shoulders and gently pushed me back—I saw urgency in his eyes as he looked into mine. He spoke again, quietly but firmly, "Rahab, we must hurry."

FREEDOM

They gathered us together and hurried us out the door, but we all stopped and stared once we got outside. Before us was a scene we could never have imagined. Since childhood, I was accustomed to walking out and seeing mud block buildings, huts, and tents around us, surrounded by the two-story wall that enclosed the city. Above, I was used to seeing the upper wall around the upper city.

But as I stepped through the door and looked around I felt a strange feeling. Many of the buildings and tents were there as they had been, but there was no wall around us. In its place were mounds of rubble that had collapsed down the embankment forming ramps by which the army could enter the city. When I looked up to the upper levels, I saw that much of that wall had collapsed as well, providing more ramps that provided the Israelite army easy entrance to the most wealthy and secure areas of the city.

Later, I questioned the older spy—I learned his name was Ardon, son of Caleb who was one of the original 12 spies who had entered the land 40 years earlier—about the walls. He told me:

"We had viewed those walls as a major obstacle in Yahweh's plan for us. We could not see how we would get over them or through them to take the city. But suddenly, what had seemed an insurmountable barrier instantly became the primary access for our victory."

As we stepped out away from the inn, clouds of dust were hovering over the city, and all around us fires were burning … the whole city was ablaze. Beyond the mounds that had once been the lower walls I could see hills to the right and grass and trees behind us. Off in the distance I could see the fields my father and brothers had worked for years.

When you are accustomed to seeing the same site every day, and when that scene is suddenly, violently, and catastrophically changed, it dazes you. If you have ever lived through a disaster that has drastically altered the appearance of your surroundings, you know exactly what I mean. For a moment I could not move—I just stood there with my family, staring.

The spies grabbed our arms and pulled us along with them. That is when I awoke to what was happening throughout the city. As we climbed over the rubble that used to be the gate, I looked around and saw dead city guards lying in the streets throughout the city. Blood was everywhere. Israelite soldiers were now going into all of the buildings—we could hear screams throughout the city. As we were led away from the remains of the wall, the number of screams gradually lessened, then stopped.

I instantly remembered the last part of the song:

> *all the inhabitants of Canaan have melted away.*
> *Terror and dread fall upon them;*
> > *because of the greatness of your arm*
> > *they are still as stone.*

I realized at that moment that *Yahweh* was keeping the prophecy. Everyone in the city knew that ancient song. They knew what *Yahweh* had promised; and they could have turned to Him—as I had—they had so many opportunities. Instead, they insisted on calling upon their false gods, leading down that path to death and destruction.

As the spies led us away from the city I looked back and saw our house standing alone surrounded by all the rubble. It was the only section of the lower wall that had not collapsed.

Then I saw it up on the second level of the inn: that portion of the wall was still standing with the window remaining intact, and hanging in that lone window was the scarlet cord.

I collapsed to my knees in tears, with sobs of relief and gratitude erupting from deep, deep within, understanding for the first time that *Yahweh* had not abandoned me, but that He indeed remembered me—and delivered me.

CHAPTER 4

Lessons

I cannot tell you everything I learned through this experience, but I would like to share with you a few of the truths I came to understand. If you are facing the threat of doom and despair, along with all the fears and anxiety that come with those threats, perhaps these lessons will help you.

YAHWEH LOVES HIS PEOPLE DEEPLY AND IS COMMITTED TO ACCOMPLISHING HIS WONDERFUL PLAN FOR THEM ... AND NOTHING CAN STOP HIM

We would never have thought of our gods as loving us or of having a plan for our wellbeing. Instead, we believed some of them to be cruel, and we wanted to appease them so they might grant our requests. The fact that *Yahweh* had established a covenant relationship with His people based on love—His love for them and their love for Him—was a strange and entirely foreign idea for our culture. But to go further and consider that He had a rich and wonderful plan for the blessing and good of His people was completely unimaginable to us.

And then, what made it all so astounding was that He had the absolute and ultimate power to accomplish His plan for His people; and the forces of nature, or man, or other spiritual powers could do absolutely nothing to stop Him from accomplishing that wonderful plan.

We all knew the stories of His power over nature itself, using it to bring plagues upon Egypt, and of His corresponding dominance over the Egyptian gods that were supposed to control those natural forces.

The Red Sea was no match for *Yahweh* when He easily parted it so His people could pass through and escape the Egyptians; and after passing through, He commanded those very waters to utterly destroy the Egyptian army, the greatest army in the world. We knew that He defeated Pharaoh, the most powerful king in all the land. Years later, He destroyed Kings Sihon and Og and their armies when they attempted to oppose His people and hinder His plan. We had heard all of these stories for years.

Then we personally saw that the Jordan River was no match for the power and plan of *Yahweh*. The fortified walls of Jericho, along with all of the gods who were supposed to guard it, trembled and collapsed before Him in disgrace and defeat at the mere sound of trumpet blasts and shouts from His people.

These all clearly showed me that *Yahweh* had a good, wonderful, and perfect plan for His people, and that there was no natural, spiritual, or human force that could keep Him from accomplishing that plan.

But I personally saw *Yahweh*'s power and compassion at work in my own life—they were poured out on behalf of my family and me. When I turned around after our escape and saw our house standing, I realized that He had destroyed the walls surrounding Jericho but left our house standing—alone. Not only did He have the power to bring down those walls, He was able to single out one building and protect it from the surrounding destruction! That is true power. But it also showed His compassion. He did not have to save my family and me—but He did. He cared for me! A lowly prostitute! He destroyed the walls around the whole city but protected my home. He destroyed everyone in the city but saved me. He cared for me—Rahab, the harlot!

Everything seemed so bleak—it seemed human, spiritual, and natural forces were all coming together and would surely destroy me—but He did not fail me. He chose to love me, deliver me, and welcome me into His people; and I eventually came to understand His plan for me. Oh, what a wonderful God ... the One and only true God!

Perhaps you are facing intense struggles right now that tempt you to doubt His love and plan and power. You may be experiencing fear, anxiety, or panic over natural, spiritual, or human forces that threaten to destroy you. If so, please remember my story and these truths: no matter how bleak the situation and circumstances, He loves His people dearly and has ultimate power over all.

There is absolutely nothing that can keep Him from accomplishing His loving, wonderful, and perfect plan for His people. There is no force—whether human, natural, or spiritual—that can stand in His way, no matter how daunting, massive, powerful, or terrifying they may seem. Indeed, every obstacle that presents itself before Yahweh to oppose Him and His perfect plan will eventually and ultimately crumble at His feet in disgrace and defeat, just like the walls of Jericho, becoming the ramp by which He conquers and delivers.

If you count yourself as one of His people, then do not fear, regardless of the struggle. Do not yield to the temptation to think He has forgotten or abandoned you; He has not and will not. His love, power, and plan are all at work for you, and—at just the right time—He *will* prevail. He can turn that looming threat into the pathway for His blessing. God alone can deliver you. I saw it for myself. I hope you can find peace in that truth.

2

FOLLOWING FALSE GODS DESTROYS LIVES

Looking back on my experience, I came to understand that worshipping the gods of Canaan always hurt someone. As a result, we knew nothing about showing compassion to each other. It was foreign to us and was seen as weakness; in place of showing compassion, we made victims.

Young girls were victims, women were victims; I knew from my own experience. From childhood, we learned that our value, our worth—to the gods and to men—was directly tied to our ability to perform sexually. As adults, we were expected to satisfy—sexually and as house servants. Women had no rights, no legal protection. Our only protection came from the men in our lives, either our fathers or husbands. We were little more than property, and if they chose to abuse us there was nothing we could do. Such cruelty turned a young girl's tender heart to stone.

Following those gods did this.

The men were victims, too—not in the same way, but they still suffered. Following the Canaanite gods led them to focus only on their own desires, their own lusts. It was all they thought about; it was all they talked about. Our whole city was obsessed with sex. Believe me, I saw it and heard it all the time— they came to *me*. The thirst of their lusts was unquenchable. When a boy became a man, it's almost as if he changed into an animal. He no longer cared for anyone or anything else. His lusts and cravings drove him from one twisted sexual experience to the next, never to be satisfied. When they grew tired of women and other men, they went after children, then animals. Their lives were consumed by it. They were slaves to it.

The worship of our gods encouraged this.

But the ones who suffered most were the babies. Our gods placed little value on life. They were not concerned about the helpless. The people of our land believed that offering their babies on the altar of Molech would solve all their problems. Every time a priest placed a baby in the fiery arms of that statue, he promised direction from the god it represented and deliverance from whatever threat we faced.

He was wrong. It never solved our problems. Instead it tortured and destroyed innocent lives, leaving the blood of babies on the hands of everyone in the city. Babies died needlessly in the most agonizing way you can imagine.

Looking back, I am amazed at how some people could justify the torture and destruction of innocent lives as part of their religion. What kind of god could be pleased with this?

But we were told our gods expected it.

If you are living under the fear of impending doom, beware of the temptation to follow other gods or of seeking alternatives to *Yahweh*. All such options are false; following them makes victims of the helpless, and it destroys innocent lives. God alone is worthy of our trust and devotion.

Following *Yahweh*, The True God, Is Worth Any And Every Risk

When I hid the spies, I went against everything I had ever been taught as a child and as an adult. Except for maybe some of my family members, no one else in Jericho would have taken my side. I knew I would be tortured and suffer an agonizing death if they were discovered. No one in Jericho would have understood, no one in all of Canaan would have sympathized.

And it was all so terrifying. I had never seen this *Yahweh*, I had only heard of Him. I did not know for sure that He would save me or my family. What if He chose not to save us? He never promised me anything; I only had the promise of the spies.

But that did not matter. I came to believe that *Yahweh* was the one true God. He was good, He cared for His people, He was powerful, and He opposed the practices that went along with worshipping the false gods. He opposed all the things that almost destroyed me.

I came to understand and believe that it would be better to die as a result of siding with *Yahweh* than to live ten lifetimes following and serving the false gods.

I also came to understand that following *Yahweh* could be extremely costly, but the cost could never compare to the blessings.

If you are facing crisis right now, you might be tempted to turn from Him. His workings might not make sense to you, and the temptation to turn from Him may seem overpowering. Following Him may go against everything you have learned and think you know. You may be the only one willing to take a stand, and you might be risking everything—perhaps even your own life. Following Him may seem the most painful option before you.

I understand from my own experience that doing the right thing could cost a person everything. Still, please do not give in to the temptation to turn from God. Remaining true to Him will certainly be risky, and it could be very costly; but I believe it will be the best option, and ultimately it will prove to be worth every risk and consequence. It certainly did for me.

God alone is worthy of such risks.

YAHWEH IS ABUNDANTLY MERCIFUL

Over time, I came to understand that He did not have to save me and my family. We all shared in the guilt of the atrocities that went with worshipping false gods. The people of Jericho knew the ancient stories of *Yahweh* and His commands forbidding such things, but they insisted on continuing in them. They had every opportunity to turn to Him, but they refused. They knew all of the stories of *Yahweh's* power, yet they chose to trust their own gods instead. I alone was willing to turn from our ways to Him.

But I was a poor, lowly prostitute. I had done horrible things—things I cannot bear to talk about now. I helped satisfy the lowest levels of men's revolting lusts. Of course, I did not have much to say about it in my younger years, and my circumstances bound me to that way of life. But my heart and life had been contaminated by participating in the most repulsive activities ever conceived in the deepest, darkest, most vile corners of a man's heart and mind.

Yet, He saved me.

I stood by and watched as the priests of Molech destroyed babies. Those horrible images were burned into my memory. Deep down I knew it was wrong, but I said nothing. I never actually placed any of those babies into the arms of Molech, but I was guilty by my silence. I had blood on my hands.

Yet, He saved me.

The atrocities and horrors associated with following the Canaanite gods are unimaginable to many; but they were commonplace for us—for me. I did nothing to deserve deliverance. He did not owe me a thing. I was completely unworthy.

Yet, He saved me.

He did not deliver me in the way I expected. It took seven days of marching before I was finally rescued. By the sixth day I started to wonder if He would truly rescue me, and—I am ashamed to admit—I even wondered if He was *able* to deliver me. I started to question His love and strength.

And yet, He saved me.

And He blessed me. I used to dream of marrying a good man and having children—I longed for them—but I never really expected those dreams to come true. But *Yahweh* gave me a wonderful, loving husband; Ardon, the spy who saved me, later introduced me to his friend Salmon, from the tribe of Judah, who received me as his wife.

He gave us a wonderful family and a home in the land just south of Jericho where the tribe of Judah eventually settled. I lived out my days in the arms of a man who truly loved me, not for how I could perform or please him, but as an individual, a real person. And I actually allowed myself to love a man, this man.

But His blessings did not stop there. If you read your Bible you will find that He chose to give Israel her greatest king—King David—through our family line. Can you believe it? A descendent of Rahab the prostitute reigning as the king!

And if you continue to read, you will see that He also chose to give birth to the ultimate and Almighty King of the Universe, the Messiah of Israel, through our family line—the line of a common Canaanite prostitute!

I did not deserve any of this, but in His great mercy He saved me and blessed me in ways I could never have imagined.

Are you facing threats that seem overwhelming?

Do you live in a darkness that threatens to consume you? Have you lived a life that you know has been the opposite of what He designed and desires? Do you fear that God would never listen to you? Does it seem ridiculous to think that He would ever love you or save you?

I do not know you or your situation, but I do know that *Yahweh*, my God—God alone—is a God of immeasurable and matchless mercy, love, and compassion. God alone is able to save.

He poured these out upon me; I know He would do the same for you.

And now, may His blessings and peace rest on you today, and for all time, and for that time which is beyond all time.

And may you find your comfort and rest in God alone.

Amen.

Resources for Further Study

For the walls of Jericho:

From "The Civil Engineer" — https://www.thecivilengineer.org/online-historical-database-of-civil-infrastructure/item/393-wall-of-jericho

From "Ancient Origins" — https://www.ancient-origins.net/ancient-places-asia/walls-jericho-0012893

For the sexual practices related to Canaanite paganism, do an Internet search on "Baal Orgies"

For the practice of sacrificing children to Molech, do an Internet search on "Molech child sacrifice"

About the Author

After more than 30 years in pastoral and denomi-
national ministry, in 2016 John Revell launched "Life
Line Chaplaincy, Inc.," a 501(c)(3) not-for-profit corporation in Connecticut. He currently serves as chap-
lain for the Stamford Police Department, Westport
Police Department, and Connecticut State Police,
but also provides on-demand chaplaincy services
for multiple police departments and first responder
agencies in Southwest Connecticut. All profits from
the sale of this book go to help provide chaplaincy
services for first responders. For more information,
go to LLChaplaincy.org.

Discussion
Guide

1. Do you know anyone who can relate to Rahab's abuse and having been objectified by men? If so, have they reflected any of Rahab's attitudes?

2. What components of our nation and/or culture might reflect some of the values and patterns displayed in Jericho?

Discussion Guide

3. What aspects of our current situation might produce the same levels of panic and alarm reflected in Jericho?

Discussion
Guide

4. What are some personal crises that could produce the same levels of panic?

Discussion
Guide

5. When Rahab chose to embrace Yahweh and protect the spies, she was placing herself and her family at serious risk. What kinds of commitments or convictions might God's people face today that could put them at serious risk?

Discussion Guide

6. Rahab is heralded in Hebrews 11 as one of the great heroes of faith, but there was nothing glamorous about her decision at the time. What are some situations in which we may be called to exercise faith when it might not appear glamorous or "spiritual"?

Discussion Guide

7.   God showed extraordinary levels of mercy toward Rahab; what evidences of His extreme mercy have you observed in your own life?

Discussion Guide

8. God's miraculous intervention with the Jordan river and His destruction of Jericho's wall demonstrated His willingness and power to take extreme, unexpected measures in order to accomplish His loving will and plan for His people. How have you seen Him act in extreme levels of love and power to accomplish His will and plan for you?

CPSIA information can be obtained
at www.ICGtesting.com
Printed in the USA
LVHW090120201020
669248LV00006B/155

9 780975 412046